when I heard
the learn'd astronomer

words by **Walt Whitman**   pictures by **Loren Long**

SIMON & SCHUSTER BOOKS FOR YOUNG READERS • An imprint of Simon & Schuster Children's Publishing Division • 1230 Avenue of the Americas, New York, New York 10020 • Illustrations copyright © 2004 by Loren Long • All rights reserved, including the right of reproduction in whole or in part in any form. • SIMON & SCHUSTER BOOKS FOR YOUNG READERS is a trademark of Simon & Schuster, Inc. • Book design by Dan Potash • The text for this book is set in Blue Century. • The illustrations for this book are rendered in acrylics. • Manufactured in the United States of America

2 4 6 8 10 9 7 5 3 1

CIP data for this book is available from the Library of Congress. • ISBN 0-689-86397-7

Simon & Schuster Books for Young Readers

NEW YORK   LONDON   TORONTO   SYDNEY

To Caleb, who is brave and strong

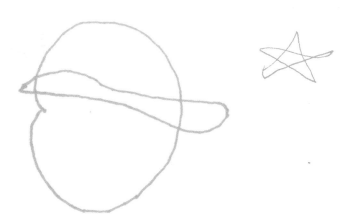

When I heard the learn'd astronomer;

When the proofs, the figures, were ranged in columns before me;

$$\frac{a}{d} = \frac{1}{3}, \qquad \frac{d}{c} = \frac{9}{5} \quad \land \atop \lor \quad = \frac{5}{6}$$

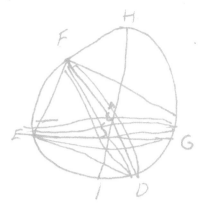

When I was shown the charts and the diagrams,
to add, divide, and measure them;

When I, sitting, heard the astronomer,
where he lectured with much applause in the lecture-room,

How soon, unaccountable, I became tired and sick;

Till rising and gliding out, I wander'd off by myself,

In the mystical moist night-air,

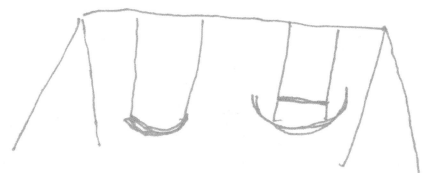

and from time to time,

Look'd up in perfect silence at the stars.

"Imagination is more important than knowledge. Knowledge is limited. Imagination encircles the world."
—Albert Einstein

The line drawings used on the front flap, back jacket, and throughout
the pages of this book were created by Griffith and Graham Long.